KEYS TO CHURCH
PLANTING MOVEMENTS

THE ADVENTURES OF STEPHANAS:
FIRST CENTURY DISCIPLE

By K. Sutter
Illustrated by S. Sutter

Keys to Church Planting Movements

Second Printing 2008

Cover Art by S. Sutter

Editing by Brian Hogan and K. Sutter

Published by Asteroidea Books

Printed by Edwards Brothers, Ann Arbor, MI in USA

ISBN 978–0–9799056–3–6

FOREWORD

Here is much–needed spiritual "tune–up" for church planters! Several good books on church planting have appeared in the last few years with much of the same material as older books, having given only new order and names to old concepts. But Sutter's Keys to Church Planting Movements adds refreshingly new insights to proven procedures:

- He clarifies universally applicable guidelines, avoiding a 'universal formula' for all cultures.

- He uses words that ordinary mortals under-stand, avoiding missions jargon and code words.

- He integrates both sources of divine guidance to multiply God's flocks, relying on the Holy Spirit and on God's Word.

- He warns of common pitfalls for church plan-ters, evangelists and new church leaders with-out being negative.

- He leaves options open to start different kinds of churches for fields with different needs and expectations.

- His advice reaches both heaven and earth, linking Christ's authority to practical, easy–to–do guidelines for field workers.

- His guidelines do not require large budgets nor advanced academic degrees.

- He covers all essential bases from preparing church planters to training new church leaders who develop the ministries that the New Testament requires.

- He does not add man–made rules to biblical requirements for leaders, churches or baptism and etc.

I have worked with the author in a church planting project and co–taught with him to train leaders. He is one of the most caring, spontaneous and simply fun persons that I know, and his book reflects these qualities. Read it, heed it, and be blessed!

George Patterson

TABLE OF CONTENTS

INTRODUCTION: Finding the
KEYS 🔑

"These who have turned the world upside down have come here too...."[1] Jesus' disciples rocked the world in the first century! The transforming, life–giving, community–changing, nation–building power of the Gospel spread like wildfire. How do we make the same kind of impact upon our world today?

Can we find a simple "how to" book for making disciples among the world's remaining unreached tribes and nations? Many tasks can be accomplished by following a list of directions. For example, to bake a loaf of bread, we follow a recipe, adding the right ingredients in the right order. For assembling a new bicycle, we have written instructions to lead us through the process. In planning a new project, we try to figure out the sequence so we can move along step by step, from start to finish. However, when it comes to helping people, you can forget orderly sequences. God doesn't seem to like formulas very much either. He wants us to depend upon His Spirit and His Word.

Help comes as we study the New Testament and find key principles. We are about to look at Biblical principles for multiplying churches among unreached peoples. The logical way is to present the keys in a linear fashion, from beginning to end. The danger in this is that we then expect our actual work to follow the same progression, step–by–step. We may worry so much about doing something out of sequence, that we miss the leading of the Holy Spirit!

Avoid thinking in terms of steps to be followed: 1, 2, 3, 4.... Rather, let's look at these key church planting principles as actual, literal keys designed to unlock specific doors. Think of all the keys (we'll identify 26 of them) attached to one big key ring. As we move into pioneer church planting, we will carry our keys along. We may find that many doors are already swung wide open. No need for a key if the door is open. Keys are only necessary for unlocking closed doors.

Imagine being a church planter who arrives on the field and immediately discovers a small, healthy fellowship already formed. The leader speaks your language and tells you the church is eager to multiply and reach their people. He asks, "We're not sure what to do, will you help?" What joy! The process is well underway! You would not go to "step number one." You would join God in what He is already doing—He is the "Master Key"—and use whatever other keys might be needed as He leads you and these local believers forward.

Expect things to come out of sequence. There will be overlap. Many things happen simultaneously. By becoming familiar with the keys, you'll know what to use, when, as you unlock church planting movements among the unreached.

Effectively communicating these key principles across educational, cultural and linguistic boundaries has meant getting down to the basics and saying it in easy to remember ways. I've tried to keep it simple, brief and to the point.

To better understand New Testament keys to unlocking church planning movements among the unreached, we are going back in time to the first century A.D., when these keys were first used. As we do this, please be sure to check the endnotes after each section, for input on applying the principles today. Although these principles are 2,000 years old, every one of them is vital and relevant for today! [2]

Let's learn from the experiences of a fictitious first–century disciple named Stephanas (not to be confused with Stephen in the Book of Acts). Stephanas simply follows the example of Jesus and the apostles as he plants churches among people of another culture.

[1] Acts 17:6, New King James Version
[2] Thank you to Dr. George Patterson and Brian Hogan for their influence and help: George for lovingly mentoring and inspiring me in church planting; Brian for working closely with me in making the teaching easy to understand and pass on to others.

🔑SEE God's purpose to bless and transform all nations

Stephanas was a Gentile. His people first heard the Good News from Jewish believers reaching out to them cross–culturally. Shortly after beginning to follow Jesus and joining a church in his neighbor's home, Stephanas learned that God wanted not only to bless him and his people, but through him God wanted to reach and bless others. In fact God's central purpose is to reach every tongue, tribe and nation with the transforming power of the Gospel!

Jesus said "And this gospel of the kingdom will be preached in the whole world as testimony to all nations and, then the end will come."[1] [2] Stephanas was convinced that before Jesus' return, the nations must first be reached with the Gospel. He knew the job was not finished.[3]

Jesus commissioned His followers to go to all nations and do the following: [4]

- **Make disciples**

- **Baptize them**

- **Teach them to obey all He commanded**

Paul, the Apostle, was Stephanas' role model. Paul went out and did just what Jesus said to do. Luke, one of Paul's friends and co-workers recorded some of Paul and Barnabas's exploits: "They preached the good news in that city and won a large number of disciples. Then they returned to Lystra, Iconium and Antioch, strengthening the disciples and encouraging them to remain true to the faith. 'We must go through many hardships to enter the kingdom of God,' they said. Paul and Barnabas appointed elders for them in each church and, with prayer and fasting, committed them to the Lord, in whom they had put their trust."[5] Stephanas recognized that Paul and his team did three basic things as they obeyed the great commission:

- **Evangelism** *("preached the good news")*

- **Discipleship** ("strengthening the disciples and encouraging them to remain true to the faith")

- **Leadership Training** ("appointed elders")

---

[1] Matthew 24:14

[2] The word "nations" comes from the Greek word "ethne." Jesus was referring to ethnic groups or "people groups" rather than geopolitical countries. A "people group" is defined as: "A significantly large ethno-linguistic grouping of people who perceive themselves to have a common affinity to one another. From the viewpoint of world evangelization, this is the largest group within which the gospel can spread as a church planting movement (people movement) without encountering barriers of understanding." An "un-reached people group" is defined as: "A people group

within which there is no indigenous community of believing Christians with adequate numbers and resources to evangelize the people group without requiring outside (cross-cultural) assistance."

[3] How close are we today to fulfilling God's goal, nearly 2,000 years later? It is calculated that there are about 27,000 people groups in the world. We have reached about 14,000 with the gospel, but 13,000 people groups are still unreached. Therefore YWAM leader, Fred Markert, says we have 1000s of reasons why Jesus has not yet returned.

[4] Matthew 28:18-20
[5] Acts 14:21-23

⚷ BELIEVE in the Church's potential to reproduce and cover the earth

Stephanas remembered what Jesus told His disciples: "But you will receive power when the Holy Spirit comes on you; and you will be my witnesses in Jerusalem, and in all Judea and Samaria, and to the ends of the earth."[1] He imagined what churches might look like as the Holy Spirit multiplied them from culture to culture.

Stephanas would not have envisioned planting only one single, individual, isolated church. His goal was to plant the only kinds of churches he was familiar with: simple ones which reproduce from house to house into daughter, granddaughter and great–granddaughter churches—what we call today, a Church Planting Movement (CPM).

Jesus often used seeds to illustrate the reproductive power of the Kingdom of God. Stephanas considered the wheat growing in the fields near his home. A church is like a grain of wheat; after it is planted, it grows and reproduces. When planted, one grain of wheat usually produces about 25 grains. He figured out the potential for multiplication.

Assuming two plantings per year, one grain of wheat could produce—

> **Year I** – 1ST season: 1 grain X 25 = 25
> 2ND season: 25 X 25 = 625
>
> **Year II** – 1ST season: 625 X 25 = 15,625
> 2ND season: 15,625 X 25 = 390,625
>
> **Year III** – 1ST season: 390,625 X 25 = 9,765,625
> 2ND season: 9,765,625 X 25 = 244,140,625

> —producing more than enough wheat to feed the whole Roman Empire. Add a few more years . . . the entire world is full of wheat!

Jesus told a parable of the Growing Seed: "This is what the Kingdom of God is like. A man scatters seed on the ground. Night and day, whether he sleeps or gets up, the seed sprouts and grows, though he does not know how. All by itself the soil produces grain—first the stalk, then the head, then the full kernel in the head. As soon as the grain is ripe he puts the sickle to it, because the harvest has come."[2] Stephanas realized:

- God uses people to scatter the seed.

- The seed contains life, growth and reproductive power.

- Once the seed is planted, the farmer rested, trusting in God to do His part.

- This same power to reproduce is *within* the church – it is like a living organism!

- We each have our part to play, but it is God who brings the fruit. We cannot force growth and multiplication. In one of Paul's letters he wrote, "I planted the seed, Apollos watered it, but God made it grow."[3]

Stephanas thought to himself, "Ah, how wonderful to see churches multiplying across the whole earth. It *is* possible! In fact it will happen. The Hebrew Prophet Habakkuk declared, 'For the earth will be filled with the knowledge of the glory of the LORD, as the waters cover the sea.'" [4]

---

[1] Acts 1:8
[2] Mark 4:26-29
[3] I Corinthians 3:6
[4] Habakkuk 2:14

⚷ **PRAY** and ask God about your role in planting the church among the unreached

Stephanas learned the vital importance of prayer through experiences in the church that met in his neighbors' home. God answered their specific prayers for boldness in proclaiming the Gospel as well as prayers for healing and miracles. They were inspired by a report about the Jerusalem church, which, after praying in the same way, God responded with an earthquake and everyone was filled afresh with the Holy Spirit![1] [2]

PRAY and ask God about your role in planting the church among the unreached

Following Jesus' instructions, the church faithfully prayed to "the Lord of the harvest...to send out workers into His harvest field."[3]

Everybody in the church was encouraged to pray to discover how God wanted to use him or her in helping the church to grow and multiply. God would reveal to each person the part they had to play if they would simply pray and do what He said.

To be commissioned and sent away by the church to plant new churches among an unreached people group, it was important to have a clear call from God. Although Stephanas gained ministry experience through his active participation in the church, which met in his neighbors' home, he wanted to be confident that it was God leading him to another land and culture.

God speaks to His people through:

 The Scriptures

Prayer

Circumstances

His Church

— to reveal Himself, His Purpose, and His Ways. [4]

Paul the Apostle was a living example to Stephanas of a fruitful, cross–cultural church planter. Paul seemed to have a view of divine guidance consisting of three levels; each level supported and gave direction to the next. Paul understood God's will through:

1. *The Scriptures and flow of God's work in history.* Paul knew God's unchanging purpose and promise: "all the nations shall be blessed…."[5] He used Scripture to confirm his guidance to work to reach the nations. [6]

2. *A life mission.* Paul knew his life's mission. He put it in writing: "…proclaiming the gospel of God, so that the Gentiles might become an offering acceptable to God, sanctified by the Holy Spirit." [7]

3. *Seeking day–to–day guidance from God about what to do next.* Paul seemed to have confusion sometimes in this area. On one occasion his decision to visit some believers was frustrated by the devil.[8] Another time the Spirit of God blocked two well–intended ministry projects until clarity was finally reached.[9] A group of disciples, moved by the Spirit, urged him not to go to Jerusalem, yet they could not get him to change his mind.[10]

Apparently Paul was not always completely sure of the next step. In a funny way, this encouraged Stephanas. He realized that Paul was a lot like him and most other believers—he occasionally struggled to know the right decision in the short–term.

Stephanas believed that if he made choices based only on the third level of day–to–day guidance, without the foundational levels of God's purpose and his own life mission, he would not make long–term progress. Stephanas made it a habit to evaluate his immediate choices (level 3) in light of his life calling (level 2). Likewise, he tested his life calling by Scripture (level 1). When he experienced occasional difficulty with short–term guidance, he had confidence God would direct his path toward a life of increasing fruitfulness.[11] [12]

----

[1] Acts 4:31

[2] **Extraordinary Prayer:** A UNIVERSAL ELEMENT IN CHURCH PLANTING MOVEMENTS "Prayer has been foundational to every Church Planting Movement we have observed," reports David Garrison in his out-standing booklet, **Church Planting Movements**. After surveying Church Planting Movements spreading among unreached peoples around the world today, he identifies ten universal elements present in every one of them. With Garrison's permission, we will point out each of these ten universal elements as we go through the keys. Garrison and the IMB have generously made the booklet available as a free download.

www.churchplantingmovements.com Since the publication of his booklet in 2000, many more church planting movements have surfaced in all corners of the globe! Researchers are tracking over thirty of them. As follow-up, Garrison recently wrote a new book, **Church Planting Movements, _How God is Redeeming a Lost World_**, filled with faith-building, exciting stories and expanded, practical insight. Order a copy through the website above.

[3] Luke 10:2b

[4] EXPERIENCING GOD: Knowing and Doing the Will of God, written by veteran church planter Henry Blackaby, is a must for all church planters. This study helps you to: know when God is speaking, find out where God is working and join Him and experience God doing through you what only God can do! Order EXPERIENCING GOD from LifeWay Press, 127 Ninth Ave. North, Nashville, Tennessee 37234 USA. or call 1 800 458 2772.

[5] Galatians 3:8

[6] Romans 15:8-12

[7] Romans 15:16

[8] I Thessalonians 2:17-18

[9] Acts 16:6-10

[10] Acts 21:3-4, 11-14

[11] Proverbs 3:4-5

[12] "The Three Levels of Guidance", taught by YWAM leader, Jim Stier at a church planters conference in Athens, Greece

🔑 PLAN for a Church Planting Movement

Stephanas realized that it was people with *clarity of purpose* who planted churches among the unreached. They knew what God wanted them to do—they had a strategy!

As he prepared to go, Stephanas worked at writing down his vision. His goal could be described as: "an indigenous movement of spontaneously multiplying churches."

Here is what he meant:

Indigenous

Well adapted to the local community, reflecting its language and culture. An indigenous church is generated from within; supported by the local people, led by the local people, and grows as a result of the faith and obedience of the local people.

Movements

The people move together toward a common vision and goals. It is self–propelled and alive.

Spontaneously multiplying

Growth occurs without being pushed from the outside. When churches plant their own churches, multiplication increases more rapidly and the movement gains momentum.

Churches

Three simple definitions:

- ❖ Vibrant families of Jesus who listen to Him, do what He says and help others do the same
- ❖ People moving together under the Lordship of Christ
- ❖ Groups of believers of any size, committed to one another and to obeying Jesus' commands

While Stephanas' goal described what he planned to achieve within the people group he would go to, his strategy described how he intend to achieve it. He trusted God to lead by His Word and His Spirit. He learned principles from Scripture and the apostles' teaching.[1] These principles for planting churches would apply in every context; however he also knew that the methods would differ from culture to culture.

Stephanas intended to follow the basic instructions Jesus gave to the 12 apostles [2] and later the 72 disciples [3] when He sent them throughout Judea spreading His message.

Jesus told them:

- Team–up [4]

- Pray [5]

- Go! [6]

- Look for a person who welcomes you into the house [7]

- Stay with the family, eating and drinking[8]

- Heal the sick [9]

- Tell them of the kingdom of God [10]

- (From this household, new disciples might be made and fellow workers raised up who reach their own villages and beyond. This would be an answer to prayer to "the Lord of the harvest to send out workers into His harvest.")

- Waste no time if people are not open; look for another who welcomes you [11]

The 72 returned with joy.

Jesus was filled with joy.[12]

Stephanas' strategy would be:

- Scriptural
(Following the pattern used by Jesus[13], Peter[14], Paul[15], etc.)

- Low–profile
(Avoiding public gatherings when authorities are too hostile)

- Inexpensive
(Most of the unreached are also quite poor)

- Simple structure
(Meeting in homes, led by local volunteers)

- Easy to imitate and pass on

Someone once said, "If you fail to plan, you plan to fail." Stephanas planned his work—now he would work his plan.

---

[1] Today of course, we have both the Old and New Testament!

[2] Luke 9:1-11

[3] Luke 10:1-24

[4] Luke 10:1 Jesus appointed 72 of His disciples and sent them out 2 by 2 to places He Himself was about to go.

[5] Luke 10:2 Jesus told them to pray for even more workers for the plentiful harvest. As they saw the ripe harvest, they were to pray for people to be set free. New workers would thereby be mobilized for the cause.

[6] Luke 10:3-4 Jesus commanded," Go!" In the first three verses, the word "go" is used twice along with the words: sent, send and sending. They went out: **D**efenseless but victorious. **D**ependent on hospitality. **D**etermined to obey Jesus.

[7] Luke 10:5-8 Jesus told them to look for persons of peace who would welcome them into their houses.

[8] Luke 10:7 Jesus told them not to move from house to house (door to door).

[9] Luke 10:9a

[10] Luke 10:9b

[11] Luke 10:10-15

[12] Luke 10:17, Luke 10:21

[13] Luke 9:1-11, Luke 10:1-24

[14] Acts 10-11:18

[15] Acts 13-28

🔑 WORK together with like–minded people

Jesus set the example when He sent out the 72 workers, two by two. All the church planters Stephanas knew always worked in teams. People with a good balance of spiritual gifts working together bear much more fruit than one person working by himself. [1]

To cover their financial needs, some of the team planned to use their trade to earn money (like the Apostle Paul, who made tents). They would also receive some financial support from their sending churches.

The churches were confident that the Holy Spirit called this team to go. They held a special gathering to commission and send them out.[2] The believers committed to pray regularly for the team. Stephanas and his team promised to maintain regular communication with their sending churches.[3]

---

[1] Luke 10:1, Acts 10:23, 11:12; Romans 12:4-8

[2] Acts 13:1-3, The Holy Spirit told the sending church in Antioch, "Set apart for me Barnabas and Saul for the work to which I have called them." Cross-cultural church planting teams need to be *set apart from* other ministry responsibilities and *set apart with* the authority to accomplish their work.

[3] Acts14:24-28

COMMIT to reaching the goals God gives

Stephanas and his team made a firm commitment to planting reproducing churches. "We *will* reach the goal God has given." [1]

They were committed to the task rather than to a time period. They would stick with it in spite of how many years it might take.[2]

They continually sought the Lord, to know the Scriptures and to hear His voice, trusting Him to lead step–by–step.

Jesus sent the 72 ahead, to places where He Himself was about to go. Stephanas prayed, "That is what we want too, Lord! Please send us where You have prepared a ripe harvest! Show us the way."[3]

---

[1] **Intentional Planting of Reproducing Churches:** A UNIVERSAL ELEMENT IN CHURCH PLANTING MOVEMENTS "One might assume that a potent combination of extraordinary prayer and abundant evangelism would naturally result in spontaneously multiplying churches. Many missionaries and church planters have held this view, and so were surprised and disappointed when multiplying new churches did *not* follow. What we found instead was that Church Planting Movements did not emerge without a deliberate commitment to plant reproducing churches." David Garrison, **Church Planting Movements,** *How God is Redeeming a Lost World*, page 181.

[2] Luke 9:62

[3] Luke 10:1-2, John 4:34-38

🗝️**FOCUS** upon one specific people group

Stephanas and his team decided it would be wiser to reach out to one specific unreached people group. The gospel will spread with the least barriers within a people group with common background and affinity to one another.[1]

If there were other receptive people groups in the area with different languages and cultures, they would try to organize more teams. [2]

The aim was a "people movement to Christ." Rather than just reaching a few isolated people, their expectation was for the Gospel to spread through households,[3] communities and eventually the whole people group. They would not pull individual people out of their circle of influence to bring them into a foreign group.

Stephanas believed it was important to seek a responsive segment of the people group, who were content with their own culture. As outsiders, the team might attract people eager merely for cultural change and material gain.[4]

The team watched to see where God was already at work among the people. They prayed that God would open their eyes to see where His harvest was ripe, and that He would lead them to those who were spiritually hungry.[5] [6]

----

[1] Acts 10:23-24 Peter goes cross-culturally to Cornelius as well as Cornelius' relatives and friends.

[2] Normally, we need a separate church planting penetration for each unreached people. A modern analogy: In the USA, the state of Minnesota is referred to as the "Land of 10,000 Lakes". If you go to Minnesota and throw a stone into one of the lakes, ripples spread out from where the stone hit. How far will those ripples go? Through all 10,000 lakes? No, they will spread to the shore of the lake that the stone was cast into – and

no further. To get ripples going in every lake, you would need a separate stone for each lake.

[3] The Greek word for "household" is "oikos." In the Graeco-Roman culture "oikos" described not only the immediate family in the home, but included friends, servants, servants' families, and even business associates. The Apostle Paul expected more than the Jailer to be saved when he said, "Believe in the Lord Jesus, and you shall be saved, you and your household." Acts 16:31

[4] Acts 10:1-2; Acts 8:18-23

[5] John 4:35

[6] Luke 10:6 Jesus told the workers He sent out two by two, to look for "a man of peace."

🔑 LEARN the language and culture

The people group to which God led the team did not speak Greek or any other language they understood. This was one of the reasons this group had not been reached yet. Before proclaiming the Gospel, Stephanas and his friends would first need to bond with the people by living with them, gaining a good grasp of their language and appreciating their culture.[1]

Following the instructions Jesus gave His 72 workers; they entered the homes of those who welcomed them, eating and drinking whatever was offered.[2]

They sought roles in their new culture that made sense to the people. They maintained attitudes of servanthood and humility. In this, they followed Jesus in his *incarnation*. After humbly emptying Himself of the privileges of God, our Lord took on the form of an ordinary person to enable us to relate well and understand Him.[3]

Cross–cultural church planters minimize the social and cultural distance between themselves and those to whom God calls them. Stephanas said to his team, "As much as possible, let's do things their way."

---

[1] A very helpful guide for learning a new language is <u>Language Acquisition Made Practical</u> by Tom and Elizabeth Brewster The book may be ordered through William Carey Library; P.O. Box 40129; Pasadena, CA 91114 USA 1-(800) MISSION The U.S. Center for World Mission says, "No single book has done so much to dispel the fear of foreign language learning. It banishes the mystery and tells you HOW to learn step by step, on your own, in an amazingly simple, easy-to-follow guide."

[2] Luke 10:7

[3] Philippians 2:5-8

🔑 **RECOGNIZE** you have entered Satan's turf

Jesus warned the 72 workers: "Go! I am sending you out like lambs among wolves." ¹ The team knew they must be discerning, aware that Satan and his demon hosts had been in control of these people for unnumbered generations. He would not release his captives without a fight.

One team member put it this way: "Our fight must not be against the people; *we are commanded to love them*! Our fight is with the one who has kept them in deception."²They were in the midst of a spiritual battle.

During the language learning time, while personal evangelism was at a minimum, the team took on spiritual warfare as their main "outreach." They prayed for their new friends that God would "open their eyes and turn them from darkness to light, and from the power of Satan to God, so that they may receive forgiveness of sins and a place among those who are sanctified by faith...."[3]

Spiritual warfare also means spiritual welfare. The team members were careful to maintain right relationships with God and with one another.

---

[1] Luke 10:3
[2] Ephesians 6:10-12
[3] Acts 26:18

🔑 RESIST the devil and establish Christ's victory

The team accepted spiritual warfare as a daily reality. They sought to grow in the disciplines of personal prayer and group intercessory prayer to wage war more effectively.[1] They were encouraged remembering Jesus' words to His 72 workers, "I saw Satan fall like lightning from heaven. I have given you authority to...overcome all the power of the enemy...." [2]

Jesus Christ had already won the victory! However, Stephanas didn't want his team to make the mistake of assuming that Christ's victory meant they would not encounter suffering. They were all aware of the kinds of things Paul and his team went through— imprisonments, beatings, stonings, shipwrecks, etc. Is this related to a higher spiritual price from pushing back the darkness?[3] Whatever the cause, suffering is a common factor in pioneering church planting movements.

Workers intent on church planting movements must always be on their guard, to watch, fight, and pray.

---

[1] Ephesians 6:13-20
[2] Luke 10:18-19
[3] Rev. 12:11-12

🔑 LOOK for 'persons of peace'

Stephanas built relationships with the local people. From the time he first entered the community he was seeking potential leaders.

Jesus set the example with people like Levi[1], the Samaritan woman[2] and Zaccheus.[3] Then He sent out 72 workers two by two and told each team to do the same, looking for a "man of peace."[4]

Stephanas and the team would follow the Lord's instructions, looking for a man or woman with these qualities:

- Receptive and hospitable
- Reputation, either good or bad[5]
- Refers church planters to his or her own circle of influence

They planned to reach heads of households, knowing that they would be potential leaders who could share the gospel with their families and friends.[6] It's important to know who the "decision makers" are in a culture's family dynamic. Regarding many cultures, someone once said, "You win a child—you win an orphan. You win a wife—you win a widow. You win a husband—you win a family."

---

[1] Luke 5:27-32

[2] John 4:7-42

[3] Luke 19:1-10

[4] Luke 10:6-7

[5] "Good soil for the Gospel is bad people." George Patterson

[6] Acts 16:31

🔑USE methods others can imitate

Growing understanding of the language and culture enabled the team to communicate spiritual truths. They used simple teaching methods. As Paul said, "I did not come with eloquence or superior wisdom...."[1]

Jesus, when sending the 72 workers throughout Judea, told them, "Carry neither money bag, knapsack, nor sandals...." [2] Stephanas took this to mean his team should also "keep it simple." They presented the message clearly and in a way that new believers would be able to imitate. Jesus' instructions also implied that the workers should not plan to stay any longer than necessary, so it was all the more important that the methods would be easy to pass on to others.[3] [4]

---

[1] I Cor. 2:1-3

[2] Luke 10:4a, New King James Version

[3] John 4:39

[4] In the 21st Century, we tend to use the latest technology. Be careful to use only methods that the local people can afford and manage themselves, otherwise they will rely upon *you* to do it. Multiplication is hindered!

🔑 **PROCLAIM** the
essentials of the Gospel in understandable ways

Following the example of the believers who first brought the Gospel to their home communities, the team proclaimed the Good News in a manner that was both culturally meaningful and plainly understood by the people. They used a balance of "words, wonders and works" to present the Good News.

- **Words:** After His resurrection, Jesus told His disciples the vital elements of the message they were to spread: "This is what is written: The Christ will suffer and rise from the dead on the third day, and repentance and forgiveness of sins will be preached in His name to all nations, beginning at Jerusalem. You are witnesses of these things." [1] This is the message Stephanas and his coworker told:

1. *Who Jesus is (The Messiah, revealed in the Scriptures[2])*

2. *His death*

3. *His resurrection*

4. *Forgiveness of sins in His name, for all who repent*

- **Wonders:** Jesus told the 72, "heal the sick who are there and tell them, 'The kingdom of God is near you.'"[3] Likewise, the team prayed for the sick to be healed and demon possessed delivered. They relied upon God for signs and wonders. Paul wrote, "our gospel came to you not simply with words, but also with power...."[4]

- **Works:** Mindful of Jesus' teaching about the Samaritan on the road to Jericho, the team showed love in practical ways—serving people through both word and deed. Compassionately meeting practical needs was an important part of their outreach. They were confident that as they modeled this kind of lifestyle, the new churches would begin to do the same.[5]

The church planting team spread the Gospel in faith, and applied the law of the harvest: "If you sow abundantly you will also reap abundantly."[6]

---

[1] Luke 24:44-48; Paul reemphasized what Jesus said in I Corinthians 15:1-4

[2] At that time Jesus meant the Old Testament. Today we have the Gospels too. We should use both.

[3] Luke 10:9

[4] I Thessalonians 1:5. Danny Lehmann says, "God designed evangelism in such a way that He won't do it without us, and we can't do it without Him."

[5] Luke 10:25-37; Galatians 2:9-10

[6] **Abundant Evangelism:** A UNIVERSAL ELEMENT IN CHURCH PLANTING MOVEMENTS "If prayer links a Church Planting Movement to God, then evangelism is its connection with the people. Essential to every movement is the principle of over-sowing. Just as nature requires a tree to drop thousands of seeds to produce a single sapling...so it is with evangelism. In Church Planting Movements we find hundreds and thousands of people hearing the gospel every day and out of this abundant sowing

(through personal and mass evangelism), a growing
harvest begins to take place." David Garrison,
Church Planting Movements, *How God is Redeeming a Lost World,* page 177.

🔑 MODEL everything you teach

Stephanas modeled the Christian walk as well as ministry skills as he mobilized the local people.[1]

Discipleship typically begins before conversion and continues indefinitely.

Stephanas once read a copy of a letter Paul wrote to the Thessalonian believers: "You know how we lived among you for your sake, you became imitators of us and of the Lord; in spite of severe suffering, you welcomed the message with the joy given by the Holy Spirit. And so you became a model to all the believers in Macedonia and Achaia—your faith in God has become known everywhere."[2] Stephanas' team planned for their example to be imitated by the new believers and they in turn would become models for others.

The team knew they must be willing to face persecution as people responded to the Gospel.[3] They would prepare the new believers for what might come. Church Planting Movements often emerge in difficult settings where conversion is not popular or socially advantageous – in fact it often leads to severe persecution or even martyrdom.[4]

---

[1] Mark 3:13-15
[2] I Thessalonians 1:5-8
[3] Acts 4:13-20
[4] Matt. 10:17-25

⚷ REVIEW your goals regularly

The team regularly and prayerfully reviewed their God–given goals and evaluated the results.[1] [2]

They evaluated everything to achieve the end–vision. The team discarded every ministry activity that would not lead to "an indigenous movement of spontaneously multiplying churches."

Looking at the team's activities, these simple questions would be asked:

1. "What is going right?"

2. "What is going wrong?" ("Is something missing? Is something confusing?")

3. "What could we do better?"

_____

[1] The "YWAM Church Planting Phases Checklist." is a helpful tool for reviewing progress. Available through YWAM Church Planting Coaches (www.cpcoaches.com).
[2] I Cor. 9:19-27

⚷REORGANIZE priorities according to needs, results, and the leading of the Holy Spirit.

The team was willing to take risks and was not afraid of making mistakes. They changed ineffective methods. Stephanas was aware that Jesus told His 72 workers not to waste time with people who were not spiritually open. If the workers' message was rejected, they were to look for others who would welcome them. [1]

Paul was known to give wise counsel to church planters, "Be very careful, then, how you live—not as unwise but as wise, making the most of every opportu-

REORGANIZE priorities according to needs, results, and the leading of the Holy Spirit.

nity, because the days are evil. Therefore do not be foolish, but understand what the Lord's will is."[2]

Cross–cultural church planting can get discouraging, but Stephanas was often encouraged to continue forward by remembering what the Lord told Joshua. "Have I not commanded you? Be strong and coura-geous! Do not be terrified; do not be discouraged, for the LORD your God is with you wherever you go." [3] [4]

---

[1] Luke 10:10-15, Acts 13:50-51 (Paul does the same.)

[2] Eph. 5:15-17

[3] Joshua 1:9

[4] The following encouraging quotes are from more recent history:

"Still I am learning." — Artist Michelangelo, at the peak of his career.

"Success is never final; failure is never fatal; it is cou-rage that counts." — Sir Winston Churchill.

"Even if you're on the right track, you'll get run over if you just sit there." — Will Rogers

🔑CALL people to repent and be baptized

Jesus commanded people: "The time has come; the kingdom of God is near. Repent and believe the good news!"[1]

Stephanas was aware that Peter followed Jesus' example. After the crowd heard Peter's message on the Day of Pentecost, they were cut to the heart and asked, "Brothers, what shall we do?" Peter replied, "Repent and be baptized, every one of you...."[2] Those who had repented, believed and received the Holy Spirit, confirmed it through baptism. The apostles counted people who were baptized that day, and realized the church had grown from 120 to over 3,000!

Likewise, Stephanas and his team baptized sincerely repentant sinners without unnecessary delays, usually the same day they professed faith. When possible, they would baptize whole families.[3] New believers were rapidly incorporated into the life and ministry of the newly born church.

---

[1] Mark 1:15
[2] Acts 2:37-38
[3] Acts 2:37-42; Acts 18:8

🔑 GATHER the new believers together

The birth of the Jerusalem church set the pattern for all the churches. Newly baptized believers were drawn into homes where "they devoted themselves to the apostles' teaching and to the fellowship, to the breaking of bread and to prayer."[1]

The team rejoiced when the first new church was born! In the beginning it had only a few people. But they knew it possessed the God–given potential to grow and reproduce!

As outsiders, Stephanas' team avoided the temptation of bringing the new believers into their team. The cross–cultural team served as "spiritual midwifes" helping in the birth of the indigenous church. As the new spiritual family formed, they tried to get out of the way.

The new church met in the homes of the local people. It was the natural place for encouraging love, prayer, accountability, giving, evangelism and ministry to one another.[2]

---

[1] Acts 2:42
[2] Acts 2:42-47

🔑 EQUIP people to be obedient to Christ's commands

Jesus said, "If you love Me, you will obey what I command."[1]

Stephanas knew that Jesus commissioned His people to go make disciples, baptize them and teach them to obey all of His commands. [2]

To insure that Jesus' basic commands were taught, the team made a list:[3]

- Repent, Believe and Receive the Holy Spirit [4]
- Be Baptized [5]
- Love [6]
- Break Bread [7]
- Pray [8]
- Give[9]
- Make Disciples [10]

The team helped the people learn from and apply the apostles teaching to their lives. They also taught the disciples how to hear the voice of the Lord in their hearts through prayer. God blesses those who *know and do* His will. Churches grow and multiply when Jesus is obeyed.[11]

While the new church stressed obedience to the commands of Jesus, they emphasized that obedience must always come from a motive of love. Any other motivation for obedience leads a church to fall into the deadly trap of legalism and dead religion.

Stephanas and his team committed themselves to never allow any human authority to prevent them or their disciples from simple, loving obedience to the commands of the Lord Jesus.[12]

[Important Note for 21st Century Church Planters After 2,000 years, the Church has accumulated a vast number of human customs which are found nowhere in the Bible. Today we must teach emerging leaders to discern the difference between mere human tradition and the commands of the New Testament. See Appendix 1, for a helpful guide.]

[1] John 14:15

[2] Matthew 28:19-20; Acts 2:37-47

[3] George Patterson writes: "Jesus ordered over forty things; we can group them under seven basic commands. In Acts 2 we see the 3,000 new believers of the first New Testament church obeying *all* of them in their basic form." Church Multiplication Guide, pg. 21.

[4] These go together; a person can't do one without the others. Mark 1:15, John 20:22.

[5] Baptism includes living forever the new, holy life it signifies. Matt. 28:19-20

[6] Love God, family, fellow disciples, neighbors, and even enemies. (forgiveness) Luke 10:25-37

[7] This includes communion with Christ and with His people. Luke 22:14-20

[8] Prayer includes listening to God speak through His Word and His Spirit. Matt. 6:5-13, Matt. 4:4

[9] Matt 6:19-21

[10] Disciple making includes: witnessing, teaching, training leaders, etc. Matt 28:18-19, Luke 24:46-48

[11] **The Authority of God's Word:** A UNIVERSAL ELEMENT IN CHURCH PLANTING MOVEMENTS "Like an invisible spinal cord aligning and supporting the movement, there runs through each Church Planting Movement a commitment to the authority of the Bible. Even among largely non-literate peoples, for whom Scripture reading is rare, believers rely heavily on audiocassettes of the Bible clinging to every word.

They have also learned to approach every faith and life situation with the question, 'How can I best glorify Christ in this situation?' In following this principle they never venture far from biblical authority. These two governing forces of biblical authority and Christ's Lordship reinforce one another like parallel railroad tracks guiding the movement as it rolls far beyond the direct control of the missionary or initial church planters." David Garrison, **Church Planting Movements, How God is Redeeming a Lost World**, page182.

[12] Acts 4:19

⚷ ENCOURAGE loving fellowship and outreach

New believers were bonded together in love. They discovered their place in God's family. A new community emerged, made of people pursuing right relationships with God, with one another, and with non–believers.[1]

The new church faithfully prayed to "the Lord of the harvest...to send out workers into His harvest field."[2] Their prayer was being answered! Workers, *from their midst*, were mobilized for outreach. They ministered to both physical and spiritual needs in their community.

The believers reached their extended families, following the webs of their own relationships. (Friends, servants, servants' families, business associates, etc. were typically considered part of the "household"—people they were responsible to reach.) [3] [4]

---

[1] If there are existing churches or denominations among the people group you work with, consider teaming-up or partnering with them only if they put Jesus' commands and church reproduction above all human policies. For example: avoid planting churches with those who prefer man-made requirements which are not in the New Testament for: baptism, serving the Lord's Supper, becoming a pastor, starting nearby daughter churches.

[2] Luke 10:2b

[3] Acts 16:31-32 "you and your household"

[4] A survey in the 1980's suggests that 80% of all people who turn to Christianity are the direct result of personal witness from a Christian friend or family member.

☞FACILITATE culturally meaningful worship forms

Stephanas' church back home followed the same basic pattern as the churches in Jerusalem, Antioch and other parts of the Mediterranean. These basic essentials hold true for every culture where the church takes root: repentance, faith, receiving the Holy Spirit, baptism, love for God and others, forgiveness, devotion to the apostle's teaching (God's Word), gathering for communion, prayer, fellowship, giving, discipleship, evangelism, etc.[1] However the way these activities were carried out, often differed from place to place, culture to culture.

The believers were encouraged to create their own culturally relevant worship forms, which incorporated the essentials modeled by the apostles. As with all Gentile churches, there was no requirement to adopt the culture of Jewish believers.[2] Neither were they expected to import all the cultural forms from Gentile churches in places like Antioch, Syria and Cilicia.[3]

The team used the following guidelines to help them avoid imposing their own culture upon the new church —

1. Discern the difference between divine commands and cultural preferences.[4]

2. Follow the local cultural ways as much as possible. Do not alienate the people.

3. Let the people create their own music and use their own style.

4. Encourage the new church to celebrate special local holidays and rites of passage in creative and God–honoring ways.

---

[1] Examine the New Testament model in Acts 2:37-47
[2] Acts 15
[3] I Cor. 9:22; Romans 14:4-6
[4] See Appendix 1

🗝️ **GIVE** opportunities for all to actively participate

Church gatherings were simple and meant to build up the believers and inspire worship of God. In just a few sentences, Paul summarized: "What then shall we say, brothers? When you come together, everyone has a hymn, or a word of instruction, a revelation, a tongue or an interpretation. All of these must be done for the strengthening of the church." [1]

As Paul said, *"Everyone"* had a part to play. [2] The church discovered that all believers have spiritual gifts provided by God for ministering to one another and for reaching the lost. Working together as a body, they grew.[3]

Some of the more mature believers helped provide direction for the church. As new people came to meetings, they saw these "elders" serving as leaders. Stephanas and his team avoided pastoring or leading the new church.[4]

---

[1] I Corinthians 14:26
[2] Luke 10:21
[3] Eph.4:11-16; I Cor. 12:7, 14:26
[4] Titus 1:5

⚷CONCENTRATE
efforts on mobilizing potential leaders

The team kept praying that the Lord would raise up workers for His harvest and they watched expectantly as He did it. [1]

"Work yourself out of a job" was Stephanas' mentality. He encouraged all believers to step out in evangelism, in discipling new believers, in starting new house churches, etc. He would tell them, "You have seen us do these things, but we believe you can do a better job! We cannot stay. We must go home, but this *is* your home, your people." Those who followed through—who took initiative—were recognized as potential leaders and more time was devoted to helping with their progress.[2] [3]

The team was careful not to develop the church around themselves. They kept themselves from being in the center because they knew their task was temporary. They viewed a cross–cultural church planting team's purpose as a being similar to a birds' nest. Once the young fly on their own, the nest is no longer needed.[4] The team would quickly move on as the indigenous church emerged.

Soon it would be time to withdraw. If not, the local leaders might not have taken responsibility, thinking that the team would do everything. [5] Dependency is a serious threat to the development new churches. [6] The churches found through experience, that they could trust God for all of their needs. [7]

Stephanas modeled and developed non–authoritarian, servant leadership. Servant leaders lead rather than drive their flocks.[8]

---

[1] Luke 10:2b
[2] Exodus 18:13-27

[3] "In many ways, the formation and training (of local leaders) is the most important aspect of church planting." David Hesselgrave, Planting Churches Cross-Culturally

[4] John 12:24

[5] For an excellent guide to closure and planned withdrawal read: Passing the Baton: Church Planting that Empowers by Tom Steffen. Available from William Carey Library.

[6] Avoid dependence upon foreign finances in the development of new churches. For information and practical assistance with the thorny problem of dependency contact: World Mission Associates; 825 Darby Lane; Lancaster, PA 17601-2009 USA. Ph:1 800-230-5265. WMUSA@xc.org

[7] II Cor. 8:2-3, 9:10-11

[8] Matt. 20:25-28; I Peter 5:1-4

🗝️MULTIPLY clusters
of churches

Stephanas described a healthy church planting movement as a growing vine, putting down new roots as it continues to spread and cover the land. It is not like an individual, isolated potted plant.

The team and the new leaders worked toward multiplying clusters of closely–knit house churches.[1] [2] One lone church seldom survives long. For special occasions, they arranged united gatherings of these groups.[3]

To maintain momentum, they kept a balance of ongoing evangelism, discipleship and leadership training.

[1] **House Churches:** A UNIVERSAL ELEMENT IN CHURCH PLANTING MOVEMENTS "The churches in Church Planting Movements begin as small fellowships of believers meeting in natural settings such as homes or their equivalent. Among the Maasai (Kenya), the meetings take place under trees, among the Kui (India), in open courtyards. The key element in each of these Church Planting Movements was a beginning with an intimate community of believers who were not immediately saddled with the expense or upkeep of a church building."

"Meeting in small groups certainly has economic implications. Liberating the fledgling movement from the burden of financing a building and professional clergy is no small obstacle to overcome. But there is more. House churches create an atmosphere that fosters Church Planting Movement formation. Consider the following benefits:

1. Leadership responsibilities remain small and manageable.

2. If heresies do occur they are confined by the small size of the house church, like a leak that appears in the hull of a great ship, the heresy can be sealed off in a single compartment without endangering the whole.

3. You can't hide in a small group, so accountability is amplified.

4. Member care is easier, because everyone knows everyone.

5. Because house church structure is simple, it is easier to reproduce.

6. Small groups tend to be much more efficient at evangelism and assimilation of new believers.

7. Meeting in homes positions the church closer to the lost.

8. House churches blend into the community rendering them less visible to persecutors.

9. Basing in the home keeps the church's attention on daily life issues.

10. The very nature of rapidly multiplying house churches promotes the rapid development of new church leaders."

David Garrison, Church Planting Movements, *How God is Redeeming a Lost World*, pages 191-193.

[2] It is estimated that 80 million people gather in house churches throughout China!
[3] Acts 2:46, 20:20

🗝 COACH new leaders "on–the–job"

The relationship between Paul and Timothy was famous, known by churches from Jerusalem to Rome. Stephanas and his team followed Paul's example of personal, loving and edifying relationships for the ongoing training of leaders.

Training for the development of local elders and church planters was done "on–the–job."[1] [2]

As much as possible, the training was done "behind the scenes." This approach allowed the locals to lead their own people.[3] However, it required lots of self–control and humility for Stephanas and his team members. It was sometimes hard to release less experienced local people to do the work rather than just doing the job themselves. But if the team became known as the main leaders of the movement, it would have been extremely difficult for them to later take support roles.[4]

The emphasis was "learn–by–doing." The training method for the church movement is summed up in these four words:

- **Model.** The trainer demonstrates the skill (in real–life situations)
- **Assist.** The trainer assists the trainee as he does it
- **Watch.** The trainer observes the trainee doing it on his own
- **Leave.** The trainer exits, as the new leader continues

The training was aimed at multiplying leaders. Paul's letter to Timothy illustrates the process: "You then, my son, be strong in the grace that is in Christ Jesus. And the things you have heard me say in the presence of many witnesses entrust to reliable men who will also be qualified to teach others." [5] Timothy, one of several men trained in ministry by Paul, was told to train some reliable men as well. The men trained by Timothy then taught other leaders also.[6]

Local leaders worked at encouraging and equipping all the people to join in building up the church, reaching the lost and transforming their community.[7] These leaders were carpenters, fishermen and merchants who continued in their jobs as they served the Lord in ministry.[8]

As with the Apostle Paul, the team considered the churches unfinished until local elders were appointed.[9] Leaders with proven Christ–like character and fruitfulness in ministry were selected as elders to oversee the churches. They were commissioned and prayed for in a special gathering.[10]

---

[1] Today we have the tempation of sending potential leaders away to outside institutions. This is risky when working with an unreached people group. Those who travel away to another culture, or from a rural to an urban setting or from a developing country to a developed country often do not return or do not easily fit back into the culture. Train indigenous leaders locally "**in** the ministry rather than **for** the ministry."

[2] John Wesley, though a man with many years of formal education and training, did not rely upon the schools of his day to find pastors. He said, "Give me 12 men who love Jesus with all their hearts and who do not fear men or devils and I care not one whit whether they be clergy or laity, with these men I will change the world."

Wesley put one in five people into significant leadership roles. He mobilized thousands of poor, uneducated men and women with spiritual gifts and hearts to serve, resulting in one of the greatest revivals and church planting movements in history!

[3] Acts 18:26

[4] **Local Leadership:** A UNIVERSAL ELEMENT IN CHURCH PLANTING MOVEMENTS "Missionaries involved in Church Planting Movements often speak of the self-discipline required to mentor church planters rather than do the job of church planting themselves…. This is not to say that missionaries have no role in church planting. On the contrary, local church planters receive their best training by watching how the missionary models participative Bible studies with non-Christian seekers. Walking alongside local church planters is the first step in cultivating and establishing local leadership. David Garrison, **Church Planting Movements**, page 34.

[5] II Timothy 2:1-2

[6] Effective on-the-job training courses designed to help reproduce indigenous leaders and churches are available. Both The Shepherd's Storybook and Train & Multiply combine three important elements: 1.) evangelism/leadership in real life situations; 2.) home study with simple practical studies; 3.) regular meetings between the trainer and his trainees. For these excellent resources and more go to www.Paul-Timothy.net,

www.TrainandMultiply.com and
www.MentorandMultiply.com

[7] Eph. 4:11-16

[8] **Lay Leadership:** A UNIVERSAL ELEMENT IN CHURCH PLANTING MOVEMENTS "Church Planting Movements are driven by lay leaders. These lay leaders are typically bi-vocational and come from the general profile of the people group being reached. In other words, if the people group is primarily non-literate, then the leadership shares this characteristic. If the people are primarily fishermen, so too are their lay leaders." David Garrison, **Church Planting Movements**, page 35.

[9] Titus 1:5-9

[10] Acts 14:23

DEPART as local leaders continue—at any cost—to reproduce new leaders and churches

Relying upon locally trained leaders ensured the new movement had a continual supply of potential church planters and church leaders.[1] [2]

The movement formed its own missionary teams to go reproduce churches cross–culturally.[3] [4]

As in an Olympic relay race, the "baton" of leadership for the new church planting movement was passed on to the local leaders.

The churches hosted a special farewell event for Stephanas and his team. Amid worship, prayer and tears, Stephanas commended the churches into God's hands. The team waved good–bye as they walked down the road, trusting the Holy Spirit to direct and empower the indigenous leaders to continue, whatever the cost, to reproduce new leaders and churches who would disciple their nation and go beyond to other nations.[5]

Their work completed, Stephanas and his team returned home and reported to their church. They all celebrated and thanked God together. The Lord had used them to bring the blessings of His Kingdom to a nation who had never heard! [6]

---

[1] II Chronicles 17:7-9; II Tim 2:2

[2] Dependence upon Bible College or seminary-trained leaders will mean a church planting movement will always face a shortage of leaders.

[3] Acts 10, Acts 13:1-3

[4] **Healthy Churches:** A UNIVERSAL ELEMENT IN CHURCH PLANTING MOVEMENTS "Church growth experts have written extensively in recent years about

the marks of a healthy church. Most agree that healthy churches should carry out the following five purposes: 1) worship, 2) evangelistic and missionary outreach, 3) education and discipleship, 4) ministry and 5) fellowship. In each of the Church Planting Movements we studied, these five core functions were evident."

"A number of church planters have pointed out that when these five health indicators are strong, the church can't help but grow…. The most significant one, from a missionary vantage point, is the church's missionary outreach. This impulse within these CPM-oriented churches is extending the gospel into remote people groups and overcoming barriers that have long resisted Western missionary efforts." David Garrison **Church Planting Movements**, page 36.

Garrison goes on to ask, "'Is God's glory, His true nature as revealed in the Person of Christ, evident in these Movements?' The answer is seen in the millions of changed lives, healed bodies and souls, passion for holiness, intolerance of sin, submission to God's Word, and vision to reach a lost world." **Church Planting Movements,** *How God is Redeeming a Lost World,* page 198.

[5] Acts 20:17:38
[6] Acts 14:26-28

CONCLUSION

USE THE KEYS 🔑

The original keys to unlocking church planting movements among the unreached were forged 2000 years ago. They were basic and simple, yet threw doors wide open for the powerful and rapid advance of God's Kingdom. Over time, unnecessary and often non–Scriptural changes were introduced. Church and the planting of new churches became complicated. Rather than opening doors, human methods may actually jam the locks, making them all the more difficult to open.

Let's return to "the simplicity and purity of devotion to Christ." (II Corinthians 11:3, NASB) Take these ancient keys. Use them. They still work today. Let's set the captives free!

I was launched into cross–cultural church planting in 1986 through being mentored by Dr. George Patterson. He had already planted an indigenous movement of self–reproducing churches and began equipping others to do the same. Accepting his invitation to join one of his teams, I experienced first–hand the value and joy of following New Testament principles. Eventually, with his encouragement, I began training and coaching as well. This work has taken me to six continents. From West Africa, through the Middle East and across East Asia, I have personally seen what happens when these keys are put into practice among Muslim, Hindu, Buddhist and tribal peoples.

Please continue to study the primitive, apostolic model in the Gospels and the Book of Acts, and glean more key principles. Obviously, do not try to imitate all the methods of the apostles. For example, Paul's only means of travel was to go by land or sea, he never stepped aboard a 747. We've got lots of advantages today. But rather than running off with "the latest winning methods", we should first aim at becoming "experts" in Biblical principles, using them as our standard of reference from which we develop culturally specific methods.

Working with teams throughout the world, I've seen the necessity to **adopt principles and adapt methods.** Biblical principles will work in every context, but methods must be adapted to the local situation. Listen to God for the methods He wants used in a given cultural setting. As Henry Blackaby says, "Methods don't work, God works." Understanding and applying key principles, releases us into wonderful freedom and creativity in our methods.

In closing, I'll quote a letter I received while living in Asia. My friend and co–worker, Lowell Farlow admonishes us all with these words: "Let us all walk in the fear of God as we plant churches, knowing '...we who teach will be judged more strictly.' (James 3:1) How desperately we each need an intimate relationship with the living God! Out of that relationship will come the eternal fruit of His great love and labor: the Bride of Christ—the Church."

"God Himself must be the Source and His Word the Foundation for all that we do. Knowing God and His ways gives us a context and a perspective from which to apply these principles. We must always keep our focus upon Him rather than on that which we want to do for Him."

APPENDIX 1

Important Insights for 21st Century

Church Planters

Today we must teach emerging leaders to discern the levels of authority for the activities of the church. George Patterson describes them as:

Three Levels of Authority for Church Activities

I. **New Testament Commands**. Jesus Christ requires His disciples to obey His commands. We practice them under all circumstances; we never prohibit them. Examples include: repent, believe, receive the Holy Spirit, be baptized, love God and others, break bread, pray, give, make disciples, forgive, witness for Christ, etc.

II. **New Testament Practices** (not commanded). The things the apostles did serve as examples for us, which we might or might not follow, depending on what is best for local circumstances. Examples include: holding possessions in common, laying on of hands to receive the Holy Spirit, celebrating the Lord's Supper frequently in homes and using one cup, baptizing on the day of conversion, Sunday worship, etc.

III. **Human Customs** (not mentioned in the New Testament) They have only the authority of a group's voluntary agreement (which God recognizes as binding; Matt 18:18–20). Human customs should be followed with caution. Problems come when we fail to see such traditions as man–made and temporary. We cannot force them on other congregations; we must prohibit them when they hinder obedience. Examples include: church buildings, pulpits, public invitation to raise hands or walk forward to "accept Christ", lecture–type sermons, Sunday School, preparing leaders in an academic institution outside the church, professional paid church staff, etc.

Patterson warns:" Most church divisions stem from power–hungry people who emphasize a human tradition or an apostolic practice that was not commanded, in order to secure a following. They place it on the level of a command by the force of their personality or the organization's bylaws. Painful divisions and discouragement grow out of a dogmatic attitude toward non–biblical requirements for worship, church procedures, membership, baptism, dress, ordination, pastoral training, and a dozen other things. We cancel spontaneous, loving obedience to Jesus when we confuse His authority with man–made rules."

From: <u>Church Multiplication Guide</u>, Patterson and Scoggins, pg. 29 used with permission

APPENDIX 2
Pass it on!

Pass on these keys. We have provided the drawings for you to copy and use for teaching. Below are some ideas to help introduce others to New Testament church planting principles:

The Adventures of Stephanas: First–CenturyDisciple

🗝 *Keys to Church Planting Movements*

These church planting cartoons tell the story of "Stephanas," a first–century believer, as he begins a church planting movement among an unreached people group. (Do not confuse him with Stephen, in the Book of Acts.)

Stephanas' story is told through 26 cartoons. The outline below provides the explanations for each cartoon. Each illustrates an important key in starting a church planting movement. The title for the individual picture is a key statement. All key statements begin with a verb (an *action* word) since we want people to *take action* and plant reproducing churches!

Using the cartoons and keys as an aid to training church planters:

If you make copies of the cartoons without any text, they can be used *in any language as well as with non–literate people*. This outline is intended to help with teaching the story. If you train more than 10 people, organize them into small groups. You may want to follow this format:

a) Instruct trainees to write the key statement under the picture as you tell it to them.

b) Give the accompanying scripture reference.

c) Ask, "What is happening in this picture?" Give time for responses.

d) Ask, "What does this scripture teach us?"

e) Take time for people to wait on the Lord in prayer for Him to speak through "a word of instruction, a revelation, a tongue or an interpretation." (I Corinthians 14:26)

f) Allow the group to share what God may have said

g) Give further input through teaching, examples, stories, and/or leading further discussion.

h) Be creative and encourage active participation

Begin by announcing:

The Adventures of Stephanas: First–Century Disciple

Frame a: This frame is blank so people can write the title:

"The Adventures of Stephanas:
First–Century Disciple
Keys to Church Planting Movements"

Frame b: Title picture introduces Stephanas (on the left, holding the keys, the other men are from a different culture). Explain these are like keys which unlock doors. They are to be used when needed. This is not a step–by–step list to be followed like a recipe for making bread.

Frame 1: **See God's purpose to bless and transform all nations** (Matthew 28:18–20)

Frame 2: **Believe in the Church's potential to reproduce and cover the earth** (Acts 1:8)

Frame 3: **Pray and ask God about your role in planting the church among the unreached** (John 15:4–8)

Frame 4: **Plan for a church planting movement** (Matthew 13:33)

Frame 5: **Work together with like–minded people** (Acts 15:40)

Frame 6: **Commit** to reaching the goals God gives (Luke 9:62)

Frame 7: **Focus** upon one specific people group (Acts 10)

Frame 8: **Learn** the language and culture (Philippians 2:5–7)

Frame 9: **Recognize** you have entered Satan's turf (Ephesians 6:10–12)

Frame 10: **Resist** the devil and establish Christ's victory (I Peter 5:8–10)

Frame 11: **Look** for persons of peace (Luke 10:5–7)

Frame 12: **Use** methods others can imitate (John 4:39)

Frame 13: **Proclaim** the essentials of the gospel in understandable ways (Luke 24:44–48)

Frame 14: **Model** everything you teach (I Thessalonians 1:5–8)

Frame 15: **Review** your goals regularly
(Ephesians 5:15–17)

Frame 16: **Reorganize** priorities according to needs, results and the leading of the Holy Spirit
(I Corinthians 9:24–27)

Frame 17: **Call** people to repent and be baptized
(Acts 2:37–38)

Frame 18: **Gather** the believers together
(Acts 2:41–42)

Frame 19: **Equip** people to be obedient to Jesus Christ's commands (John 14:15)

Frame 20: **Encourage** loving fellowship and outreach (Acts 2:46–47)

Frame 21: **Facilitate** culturally relevant worship
(John 4:19–24)

Frame 22: **Give** opportunities for all to actively participate (I Corinthians 14:26)

Frame 23: **Concentrate** efforts on mobilizing potential leaders (Ephesians 4:11–12)

Frame 24: **Multiply** clusters of churches
(Acts 20:20)

Frame 25: **Coach** new leaders through on–the–job training (II Timothy 2:2)

Frame 26: **Depart** as local leaders continue – at any cost – to reproduce new leaders and churches (Acts 14:21–24)

By K. Sutter, illustrations by S. Sutter

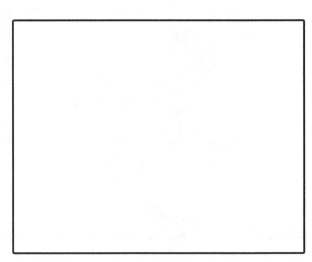

a

b

1

2

3

4

5

6

7

8

9

10

11

12

13

14

15

16

17

18

19

20

21

22

23

24

25

26

RECOMMENDED RESOURCES

The following is a brief list of books and other resources dealing with various issues related to starting church planting movements among the unreached.

Books

An Army of Ordinary People; Felicity Dale

Church Planting Movements; David Garrison*

Church Planting Movements: *How God Is Redeeming a Lost World*; David Garrison*

Church Multiplication Guide; George Patterson and Richard Scoggins*

Experiencing God: Knowing and Doing the Will of God; Henry Blackaby

Getting Started: A Practical Guide to House Church Planting; Felicity Dale

Houses that Change the World; Wolfgang Simson*

Language Acquisition Made Practical; the Brewsters*

Missionary Methods: St. Paul's or Ours?; Roland Allen*

Organic Church; Neil Cole

Passing the Baton; *Church Planting that Empowers*; Tom Steffen*

Perspectives on the World Christian Movement, A Reader; (2008) Winter / Hawthorne *

Planting Churches Cross–Culturally; Hesselgrave*

Planting Churches in Muslim Cities; Greg Livingstone *

Reproducible Pastoral Training; *Church Planting Guidelines from the Teachings of George Patterson*; O'Connor

Starting a House Church; Kreider & McClung

The Indigenous Church; Melvin L. Hodges*

The Global House Church Movement; Rad Zdero*

The Master Plan of Evangelism; Robert E. Coleman

The Starfish and the Spider: *The Unstoppable Power of Leaderless Organizations*; Ori Brafman & Rod Beckstrom

The Starfish Manifesto; Wolfgang Simson

There's a Sheep in my Bathtub: *Birth of a Mongolian Church Planting Movement*; Brian Hogan**

Rethinking the Wineskins: The Practice of the New Testament Church; Frank Viola

CD–Rom/Video/DVD

Keys to Church Planting Movements; Branch, Hogan and Sutter. This DVD training workshop includes syllabus, learning activities, skits, role plays and small group discussions.
Check for availability at CPCoaches.com

Multiplying Churches Video Workshop; George Patterson & K. Sutter team teach this interactive video workshop designed to equip pioneer church planters. Order through CPCoaches.com

The Adventures of Stephanas: *Multiplying Churches among the Unreached*; multimedia training by Brian Hogan. CD includes 30 hours of audio training with student notes, PowerPoint, electronic docs, etc.**

*Available at discount prices through:

William Carey Library
USA Credit Card orders: (800) MISSION
Outside the USA: (423) 282.9475 x299
Missionbooks.org

** Available through Asteroidea Books
AsteroideaBooks.com
info@AsteroideaBooks.com
Additional copies of Keys to Church Planting Movements by K. Sutter also available through Asteroidea Books.

Coaching and Mentoring Resources

Find simple, practical, free tools to help you with evangelism, discipleship, as well as the coaching and mentoring of church planters and leaders by visiting:

www.MentorAndMultiply.com

www.Paul–Timothy.net

www.AcquireWisdom.com

www.LK10.com

www.CPMtr.org

 YWAM Church Planting Coaches
www.CPCoaches.com

"Would you do me a favor, friends, and give special recognition to the family of Stephanas?

…I want you to honor and look up to people like that: *companions and workers who show us how to do it, giving us something to aspire to.*"

I Corinthians 16:15–16

The Message

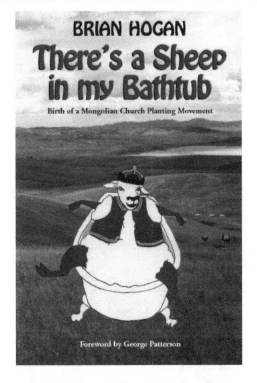

ASTEROIDEA

Books

CPSIA information can be obtained
at www.ICGtesting.com
Printed in the USA
JSHW011331090220
4102JS00001B/2